All time favourite
STORIES OF PANCHATANTRA

LITTLE SCHOLARZ PVT. LTD.

D1273033

© **LITTLE SCHOLARZ PVT LTD.**

This book first originated and published in 2014
Reprint in 2015 by
LITTLE SCHOLARZ PVT LTD.

12 - H, New Daryaganj Road, Opp. Traffic Kotwali, New Delhi - 110002 (India)
Phone # 91-11-23275124, 23275224, 23245124, Fax # 91-11-23261567
email - sales@littlescholarz.com, website - www.littlescholarz.com

Stories of Panchatantra

ISBN - 978-81-909996-0-1

Book Code - S 042   **Price: Rs. 99/- $ 3.99**

Note:- The stories narrated in the book are merely meant for the pleasure of the reader
and in no way intend to hurt the sentiments of any religious or social community.

Printed in India

CONTENTS

The Little Mice and the Big Elephants

Once upon a time, a village was ruined by a strong earthquake. The houses and roads got totally damaged. The village was shattered on the whole. Due to this, the villagers were forced to leave their houses and settle somewhere else. Finding the place vacant, the mice began to live in the ruined houses. Soon, their number grew into hundreds and thousands.

There was a big lake located near the ruined village. A herd of elephants used to visit the lake for drinking water.

A passage through the village was the only way available to them, to reach the lake. On their way to the lake, the elephants crushed hundreds of mice daily under their heavy feet. By this action of the elephants, the population of the mice was affected. The problem was getting serious day by day.

In order to find a solution to this problem, the mice held a meeting. It was decided that a request should be made to the king of the elephants regarding the problem. The King Mice met the King Elephant and said, "Sir, we live in the ruins of the village, but every time when your herd crosses the village, thousands of my subjects get crushed under their colossal feet. Kindly change your route. We promise to help you in the hour of your need, if you keep my term."

On hearing this, the King Elephant laughed and replied, "You mice are too small to be of any help to giants like us. But doesn't matter, we would favour you by changing our route to reach the lake and making you safer." The King Mice thanked the King Elephant and returned home.

One day, a group of elephant-hunters came to the lake and trapped the group of elephants in huge strong nets. The elephants struggled hard to free themselves, but all in vain. Suddenly, the king of elephants remembered the king of mice, who had promised about helping the elephants when needed. He summoned one of the elephants of his herd, which had not been trapped, to go and contact the King Mice.

On listening to the elephant, the King Mice immediately took his entire group of mice to rescue the herd. He found the elephants trapped in a thick net. The mice set themselves on the task. They nibbled the thick net at thousands of spots making it loose. The elephants broke the loose net and got free. They were grateful to the mice for their great help and became friends for ever.

Wisely said: Never underestimate people by their appearance.

The Jackal and the Drum

In a deep jungle, there lived a jackal. He had not eaten for many days and was very hungry.

"If I don't find some food soon, I will die," he thought. As he wandered through the forest in search of food, he came upon an old battlefield.

The jackal heard some noise coming at intervals from the battlefield. On hearing the noise, he thought it would be best to flee before he was attacked. But then, the braver side of him came to the surface. He decided that instead of being a coward and running off, he would find out who was making the noise.

So, gathering all his courage he moved forward. To his astonishment he found that the fighting armies had left behind an old drum that was lying near the creepers. Because of strong winds, the creepers were rubbing against it and making the noise.

The jackal continued his search for food and, nearby, he found plenty of it to last him a long time.

He was glad. As he sat down to relish the food, he thought, "I would have been a real fool if I had let a silly old war drum scare me away."

Wisely said: Only the brave succeed in life.

The Bug and the Flea

In a certain country, there lived a king who had a very beautifully decorated bedroom. An exquisite white silk sheet covered the bed and in the folds of the sheet, there lived a white flea. She used to suck the blood of the king and, in this way spent her time very happily.

One day a bug crept into the bedroom. When the flea caught sight of him, she ordered him to leave.

"Madam," said the bug, "that's not the way to speak to a guest. A guest should be made to feel welcome with sweet words and refreshments." "And besides," continued the bug, "I have sucked all types of blood, but so far I have never had the pleasure of tasting the blood of a king. I think it must be very sweet, for he has been eating the choicest food. Now, if you will permit me, I would love to taste the king's blood."

The flea said, "I only suck the king's blood when he has gone fast asleep. You are nasty and bite like a sharp needle. However, if you promise to let the king go to sleep before you start biting him, then I will let you suck his blood."

"Oh, I do promise," replied the bug. "I even swear to wait until you have sucked his blood before I suck it myself."

While they were talking, the king came and lay down on the bed.

The bug's mouth began to water and he bit the king without waiting for him to fall asleep. The bug's bite was like a sharp needle.

The king jumped up and cried out to his servants, "Something has bitten me! Search for it and kill it so that I can sleep." When the bug heard this, he hid himself in a corner of the bed.

The king's servants came and searched with sharp eyes. They found the flea lying between the folds of the sheet, and killed her.

Wisely said: Do not trust strangers.

The Fox and the Lion

Once upon a time, there was a lion and a lioness in a dense forest. They gave birth to two cubs in due course of time. The lion asked the lioness to stay at home and take care of the cubs, while he would search and bring the food.

One day, when the lion was returning home, he saw a little fox. Though the lion had not killed any animal that day, he decided not to kill the fox. "He is only a small child," he thought. Taking pity on him he took him home as a gift for the lioness. The lioness brought up the little fox as her own cub. The three young animals grew and played together.

One day, the children saw an elephant. The lion cubs wanted to fight the elephant. But the little fox was frightened and asked them to run away. So, they ran away and went to their mother.

The lion cubs told her what had happened. The lioness laughed at the little fox. At this the little fox was offended and in a rage challenged the lioness as to why she called him a coward.

The lioness replied, "My child, there is nothing wrong in eating an elephant. You feel like that only because you're not the child of a lion. You are the child of a fox. Your breed never eats elephants. Now, before the cubs recognise you to be a fox, go away from here and return to your own clan or they will kill you."

When he heard this, the young fox became frightened. He could not gather the courage to kill and eat an elephant. He decided that he should not live with the family of the lion any longer and left for the forest.

Wisely said: A coward will always remain a coward even if he is in company of the brave.

The Thief and the Brahmins

In a certain town, there lived a thief. One day, four Brahmins, from a distant part of the country, came to the same town and started selling their wares. The thief decided to rob them. He approached them and quoted very eloquently from the holy books. By doing this, he won their confidence and became their servant.

While he was in service with them, the Brahmins sold all their possessions and purchased costly jewels. In his very presence, they cut open their thighs, put all the jewels inside and then rubbed in an ointment to heal the wounds. When they prepared to leave, the thief thought, "I must travel with them. I shall poison them on the way and collect all the jewels."

He requested the four Brahmins to take pity on him and let him go with them. The Brahmins felt moved by his entreaties and took him with them.

On the way, the five of them came to a town belonging to a wild tribe. As soon as they entered the town, the crows began to scream out to the inhabitants, "Quick, quick! The rich are coming! Kill them and take their treasure!"

When the wild hunters heard the crows screaming, they rushed upon the five travellers, beat them up with cudgels, removed their clothes and searched them thoroughly. But they found nothing.

Then they said, "Travellers! Never have the crows proved to be wrong! You have got the treasure somewhere! Give it to us or we'll kill you, take off your skins and search every part of your body, until we find the treasure!"

When the thief heard this, he thought to himself, "If the wild hunters kill the Brahmins, search their bodies and take out the jewels, they will naturally kill me too. It is better that I offer my body first. Let them kill me and see that there are no jewels hidden in my body. So they will surely spare the lives of these four Brahmins, and also the jewels."

And so, having made this firm resolution the thief said to the wild hunters, "All right, then kill me first and search me!"

The wild hunters killed him and searched his body, but they found nothing. The four Brahmins were allowed to continue their journey.

Wisely said: An intelligent decision can save many lives.

The Foolish Monkey

Once upon a time, there was a king who kept a monkey as a pet. The monkey served the king in whatever way he could. No one in the kingdom dared to tease him. He had a free run of the royal household because he was the king's pet.

One hot day, the monkey sat fanning by the side of the king who was sleeping. He noticed a fly sitting on the king's chest, which disturbed the king. The monkey tried to swish her away so that the king could sleep peacefully. The fly would go away for the moment and come back again to sit on the king's chest.

The monkey could take it no longer. "I must teach the fly a lesson," he decided. He quietly left the king's room to look for a dagger to kill the fly. When he found it, he returned to the king's room. The fly was still sitting on the chest of the king. The monkey raised the dagger and brought it down with all force on the fly. The fly flew away but the king died as a result of the dagger blow delivered by the monkey.

Wisely said: Having no servant is better than keeping a foolish one.

The Two Snakes

Once upon a time, there was a king named Dasana. He had a son who was very weak and growing weaker by the day. It was found that he had a snake in his stomach.

In spite of several treatments by well-know physicians, he was not cured at all. Thoroughly fed up with his life, the prince went to a town in another kingdom, where he lived in a temple and maintained himself by begging for alms.

The king of that town had two daughters of marriageable age. One day, the king was in a bad mood. For some reason, he got very angry at the second daughter. He called his ministers and told them to marry her off to any stranger.

In compliance with the orders of the king, the ministers took her away and married her without pomp or ceremony to Dasana's son living in the old temple. The princess was very happy with the marriage and looked upon her husband as God.

Shortly after their marriage, the prince and the princess set out for another part of the country.

On the way, the princess left her husband under a tree and went into the nearby town to buy some food.

She returned to find the prince fast asleep. Suddenly, she saw a snake emerging from the prince's mouth and yet another from an anthill nearby.

The snake in the anthill said, "You wicked creature, why do you torment such a handsome prince?"

The other snake retorted, "Why are you polluting the two golden urns in your hole?"

The two carried on their conversation and a fight broke out between them.

The snake in the anthill said in anger, "Don't be arrogant. Who does not know the secret of your death? If the prince drinks a concoction made of gruel and mustard, you will die unsung."

"Oh, is that so? You will also perish if someone pours hot oil or hot water in your anthill. Don't be too proud," shot back the snake in the prince's stomach.

Thus in their row, they revealed the secrets of each other's death. The princess, who was standing behind a tree, heard their argument and came to know their secrets. She acted accordingly.

As a result, her husband recovered his health and, at the same time, they had two pots of gold to themselves.

Wisely said: Words spoken in anger may prove fatal.

The Golden Droppings

On the top of a mountain, there was a huge tree. In this tree, lived a bird whose droppings always turned into gold.

One day, a hunter came to the spot to catch birds. While he was watching, this bird discharged his droppings. The droppings hit the ground and turned into gold.

The hunter was wonder-struck and he thought to himself, "I have been catching birds since I was a small child, but never have I seen the droppings of a bird turn to gold!"

He decided to get the bird somehow. So, he set a trap in the tree. The innocent bird did not notice either the hunter or the trap and was caught. The hunter took him out of the trap and placed him in a cage.

The hunter took him home and thought, "If the king comes to know of this wonder, he will certainly take away the bird from me. Instead, I will go to the king and present this unique bird to him. He will be happy and I will get my reward."

The following day, the hunter took the bird to the king and told him everything. The king was extremely happy and told his minister to keep the bird in safe custody and feed him with the best bird food. But his minister was reluctant to accept the bird.

"Your Majesty! How can you trust the words of a hunter? Could it ever be possible to get gold from a bird's droppings! Therefore, I request you to release the bird from the cage," said the minister.

The king listened to his minister's advice and set the bird free. As soon as the door of the cage opened, the bird perched himself on a nearby doorway and fell his droppings. The droppings immediately turned into gold.

Now, even before the king could order his men to catch the bird, he flew away.

Wisely said: Check thoroughly even what seems to be impossible.

The Tiger and the Hermit

Once, a tiger was roaming carelessly among the hills and fell into a ditch in the valley. He struggled very hard to come out, but was not able to and all his efforts were in vain.

A hermit was passing by and he saw the tiger in the valley. He exclaimed, "My God! How did you fall into this?"

The tiger said, "I'll tell you later but please help me out of this first. I shall never forget your gratefulness."

The hermit collected a lot of sticks and placed them across the ditch. The tiger crawled over them and came out jumping over.

The tiger was in the ditch for a long time and was very hungry. So, on coming out of the ditch he attacked the hermit.

The hermit shouted, "Oh, stop! What are you doing? Is this my reward for saving your life?"

The tiger said, "I'm terribly hungry."

In the meantime, a frog passed by. The hermit requested the frog to do justice.

The tiger said, "To devour the prey is my right. How am I responsible for this hermit's foolishness?"

To this, the clever frog asked the tiger, "To give proper judgement, I should know where the tiger actually was?"

To this question the tiger said, "Well, look then, I was here." Saying this, the tiger jumped into the ditch.

The frog told the hermit, "O Sage, now run away to save your life, my cleverness has saved you."

The tiger again was in the ditch, licking his paw.

Wisely said: Don't show mercy to the ungrateful, lest you'll invite trouble for yourself.

The Two Headed Weaver

Once upon a time, there was a weaver by the name Mantharaka. One day, when he was weaving the cloth, the wooden frames of his loom broke. He took an axe and went to the forest to bring wood in order to make new frames.

He went round the forest but didn't find the adequate wood. From the forest, he drifted towards the seashore where he saw a huge tree. He thought that if he could cut wood from this tree, he would have enough wood for all frames for the rest of his life.

As the weaver raised his axe to cut the tree, a spirit living on that tree said, "O weaver, this tree is my home and it must be spared in any event, because it prevents my body from the cool breeze which comes from the sea."

Mantharaka said, "Sir, if I don't cut the tree and take its wood home, then my family will starve and die. So, please go somewhere else as I have to cut this tree."

The spirit answered, "If you do not cut the tree, I will give you a boon of your choice." The weaver said, "Sir, in that case, I will go home and ask my wife and friends. When I will return, you must give me what I ask for." The spirit agreed to it and the weaver returned home with joy.

While coming back to the city he met his friend, the barber, and said, "Friend, a spirit has given me a boon of my choice and gave me time to consult friends and my wife. Tell me what I should demand from him."

The barber replied, "My dear friend, demand a kingdom where you could be the King and I would be your Prime Minister. You would have a palace, where we can enjoy a luxurious life."

Mantharaka said, "True. But let me ask my wife too." The barber said, "A wise man should never ask women for advice. He can give a woman food, clothing, jewellery and above all the duties of marriage, but should never ask for advice as women think only of their own benefit and they have low wits." The weaver replied, "Even though this is true, still I would consult my wife, as she is my better half."

On reaching home, he narrated the whole story of the spirit and his boon to his wife. He also told her what the barber had advised. His wife said, "O my lord, no wise man would consult children or barbers or servants or beggars. A king's life is full of hardships. He never gets a minute's rest because anyone who rules hardly gets any time. Never envy the life of a king."

The weaver said, "You are right. But you haven't told me what boon I should choose." She answered, "Every day you are able to weave a single piece of cloth which is barely enough to meet our daily needs. You should ask for another pair of arms and another head so that you can work on two pieces of cloth at once, one in front of you, and one behind you. The first piece will help us meet our daily needs. The second one will help us meet special needs. Thus, we can live comfortably and happily."

Mantharaka agreed with his wife. He happily went to the spirit and said, "Sir, you have kindly given me a choice. I request you to give me two more hands and an extra head." He had hardly spoken before he was two-headed and four-armed.

Rejoiced, the poor weaver began his homeward journey. People on the way saw him and considering him as a kind of demon, they stoned him to death.

Wisely said: One who has no wits of one's own will perish.

The Hunter and the Doves

Once upon a time, there was a flock of doves that flew in search of food. This flock was led by their king. Once, it happened as such that the flock had flown a long distance and all the doves got tired. The king of doves encouraged the doves to fly a little more. One of the doves picked up pace and found some rice grains scattered under a banyan tree.

All the doves were happy to find the food and happily landed on the ground. As soon as they began to eat the grains, a huge net fell over them and all of them got trapped.

The doves fluttered their wings desperately trying to come out, but could not. Just then, they saw the hunter coming towards them. He appeared quite happy to find a huge number of doves trapped inside the net. The whole flock got frightened on seeing the fowler.

However, the king of doves was very intelligent and clever. He kept his patience and devised a plan to come out from this adverse situation. He said to other doves, "In order to get free from the net of this hunter, we should all fly up together clutching the net in our beak. There is strength in unity. We will decide our next course of action later. Now, come on and let's fly."

Hearing to the king, each dove picked up a portion of the huge net and they flew up together, carrying the net with them. The hunter was surprised to see the birds flying, along with the huge net. He ran after the birds, shouting madly, but could not catch them. Soon, they flew high over hills and valleys getting out of his sight.

When the King Dove saw that the hunter had given up the chase, he said to the other doves, "Now we all have to get out of this net. A mouse lives on the nearby hill. He is a good friend of mine. Let's go to him for help." They flew to a hill near a city of temples where the mouse lived.

When the mouse heard the loud noise of doves' approach, he got frightened and hid himself deeper into his hole. The King Dove gently called out to him, "Dear friend, I have come, the King Dove. We're in great difficulty. Please come out and help us." Hearing the voice of the King Dove, the mouse came out of his hole. He saw the King Dove and his friends trapped in the net. The mouse said, "Oh! Who's done all this to you?"

The King Dove explained the whole story to the mouse. He told him that they require mouse's help to nibble the net and set them free. The mouse immediately started nibbling the net around the King Dove.

The King Dove said, "No, dear. First set my followers free. A king cannot keep his subjects in pain and enjoy the freedom for himself."

The mouse understood the king's feelings and praised the king for his nobleness. As per the king's wish, the mouse nibbled first the other portion of the net and one by one all the doves were freed including the King Dove. They thanked the mouse for his help and flew away together happily to their destination.

Wisely said: Strength lies is unity.

The Gold Giving Serpent

Once upon a time, there was a poor Brahmin farmer named Haridatta. He used to work hard in the field, but could not get the result out of it. One day, after the tiring working hours, he lay down in the shade of the tree which stood in the middle of the field. Just then, he saw a terrible snake with a big hood coming out of an anthill. He thought that the serpent might be the guardian deity of the field and as he had never worshipped it, this could be the reason for the barrenness of the field.

Instantly, he brought some milk in a bowl and offered it to the serpent. While offering the milk with due regard, he addressed the serpent, "O, Guardian of this field! I didn't know that you reside here and that's why I never offered you anything. Please forgive me." Then, he went to his house.

Next day, when the poor farmer came to plough the field, he found a gold coin in the bowl near the anthill. Now, this became a regular feature of Brahmin's life. Daily he served milk to the serpent and found a gold coin.

One day, Haridatta had to go to the foreign lands. He would be away from home for a few days and so to this reason, he asked his son to take care of the serpent. The son brought the milk to the anthill and offered it to the serpent. Next day, when he came back, he found a gold coin in the bowl. After taking the gold coin, he thought, "This anthill must be full of gold coins. I will kill the serpent and take them all."

The following day, the Brahmin's son came to the field with the milk and a stick. He offered the milk to the snake and then, struck its hood with the stick. The snake escaped the blow of the stick and in a rage bit the boy to his death.

Two days later, Haridatta returned to his village and came to know about the death of his son. He grieved and mourned. But after a time, he again went to the field. He praised the snake in a loud voice and kept the milk near the anthill.

The snake came out of the anthill and said, "Brahmin, it is greed that brings you here. Now onwards, the friendship between you and me is not possible. Your son struck me in youthful ignorance and I bit him. How can I forget that stick's blow? How can you forget the pain and grief for your son who has just passed?"

Before disappearing into the anthill, the serpent gave the Brahmin a costly pearl and said, "Love, once shattered, can never be restored by a show of affection. Never come to me again." The Brahmin took the pearl and returned home, regretting the folly of his son.

Wisely said: Greed crosses all borders of reasoning and ends in disaster.

The Mice That Ate Iron

Once a merchant, who was about to set out on a journey, went to the house of a friend, taking with him an iron rod weighing two hundred tons.

"I request you to keep this iron for me," he said to his friend. "I am about to set out on a long journey, and it may be that ill luck will befall me. If so, then I can return home and sell this iron for a large price."

The friend took the iron, and even as the merchant feared, it came to pass. Misfortune overtook him on the way, and he had to return home. Straightaway he went to the house of his friend and asked him to return the iron. The friend had thought that the merchant would never return home. He did not wish to give back the costly iron, so he put on a bold face and replied, "I am sorry, my friend. The rats in my house have eaten all of the iron."

The merchant, pretending that he believed this untruth, answered promptly, "That is, indeed, sad news for me, for the iron was all that I had left. Still, I know of old rats that delight in chewing upon iron bars. I have lost much iron in the same way before, so I know how to bear my present ill luck."

This answer was very pleasing to the friend, who now was sure that the merchant believed his falsity. To avoid any further suspicion, he invited the merchant to dine with him on the morrow. The merchant accepted and went his way. As he was passing through the city, he met one of the sons of his friend. He quickly took the child home and locked him up in a room.

The next day, he went to his friend's place to dine. His friend ran out to meet him with tears streaming down his face. "You must pardon me my distress," he said to the merchant, "but yesterday one of my sons disappeared, and nothing has been heard of him since. The town-crier has been through the streets, but no trace of the child is to be found."

"I am, indeed, sorry to hear this news," replied the merchant, "for last evening I saw a sparrow hawk flying over the city with a child in its beak. The child certainly looked very much like one of your sons."

"You senseless fellow," retorted the friend, "why do you mock me in my trouble! How could a sparrow hawk carry off a child weighing twenty-three kilos?"

"Ah," replied the merchant, "you must not be surprised that a sparrow hawk should carry off a child of twenty-three kilos in our city where rats eat up two hundred tons of iron. My friend, give me back my iron, and I will gladly restore your boy."

The friend, now felt ashamed. He had tried to cheat the merchant who had put his trust in him. He immediately handed back the iron to the merchant. The merchant went home and returned with his friend's son.

Wisely said: Never break the trust of people who trust you.

The Fall and Rise of a Merchant

In the city of Vardhaman, there lived a wealthy merchant named Dhantram. He held a great reception for his wedding attended by the king, the queen, their ministers and all the rich and influential persons in the city. Present at the reception was Gopal, a lowly sweeper in the royal household. When Dhantram saw him occupying a seat reserved for the nobles of the king, he ordered his servants to throw him out of his house.

Thus insulted, Gopal thought to himself, "I am a poor man and so cannot give a fitting reply to such a wealthy person as Dhantram. I must somehow see that the king stops his favours to him." Then he hit upon a plan to take revenge from Dhantram.

One early morning, when the king was still in bed, Gopal pretending to sweep the king's bedroom began murmuring loudly, "Oh, how arrogant is Dhantram! He has the cheek to lock the queen in his embrace." Hearing this, the king demanded to know whether what Gopal was murmuring is true.

"Did Dhantram embrace the queen? " he asked.

"Oh, your majesty, I don't remember nor do I know what I was saying because I was drowsy having spent the entire night in gambling," the sweeper replied pretending to be nervous.

Not satisfied with his reply, the king thought that it was possible that the sweeper had seen Dhantram, who had equal access to the royal household as Gopal, embracing the queen. He remembered wise men saying that men were likely to talk in their sleep about what they did, saw and desired in the day. Convinced that Dhantram had indeed embraced the queen, the king barred Dhantram from entering the royal household.

The merchant began grieving his fate though he had not done any harm to the king or his relatives even in his dreams. One day, as Dhantram was trying to enter the king's palace he was barred by the king's men. Seeing this Gopal told them, "You fools, you are barring the great Dhantram who has won the king's favours. He is powerful. If you stop him, you will meet with the same fate as mine."

The merchant thought that it would bring him good to make Gopal happy and win his confidence. So, he invited the sweeper for tea and presented him with expensive clothes. He told him, "Friend, I had never meant to insult you. You had occupied a seat I had set apart for the learned. Kindly pardon me."

Pleased, the sweeper promised to win the king's favour for Dhantram again. The next day, Gopal repeated the same drama of pretending to talk irrelevantly, raving that the king was eating cucumber in the rest room. "What nonsense are you talking? Did you ever see me doing such things?" the king demanded to know. "No, your majesty. I do not know nor do I remember what I was saying because I was drowsy having spent the entire night in gambling," the sweeper said.

The king then realised that if what the sweeper had said about him was not true, then what he had said about Dhantram also could not be true. A person like Dhantram could not have done what Gopal had told. The king also found that without Dhantram the affairs of the state had suffered and civic administration had come to a standstill.

The king immediately summoned the merchant to his palace and restored to him all the authority he had enjoyed before he fell out of king's favour.

Wisely said: Respect everyone.

The Moon Lake

Once upon a time, a large herd of elephants, lived in a jungle. Their king was a huge, majestic tusker. He looked after them with love and care. Once, a severe drought hit the area. Birds and animals died of thirst.

The wild elephants suffered for want of water. Their king knew that if they did not get water soon, many of them would die of thirst. He had to find water as quickly as possible. He asked the elephants to go in different directions to look for water. One of them found a large beautiful lake full of water in another jungle far away.

The king was happy. He ordered all the elephants to make their way to the lake. Close to it was a colony of rabbits. The elephants had to pass through this colony. Thousands of rabbits got trampled to death and thousands more were injured. As the rabbits panicked, their king called a meeting.

"The herd of wild elephants have already killed and injured thousands of us. We have to take urgent steps to prevent more deaths," he said. "I want all of you to think of a way to save our race." The rabbits started thinking of ways to stop the elephants.

One rabbit stood up and said, "Your Majesty, if you will send me as your messenger to the king of the elephants, I may be able to find a solution." The king of rabbits said, "By all means, go as my messenger and see what you can do."

The little rabbit hurried out. He saw the group of elephants returning from the lake. He climbed up a huge rock and shouted, "O, king of the elephants, hear me, please."

The king of the elephants heard his voice and turned towards him. "Well, who are you?" he asked, annoyed.

"I am a messenger from the mighty Moon," replied the rabbit and continued, "But you must not be angry with me. Please remember that a messenger is never punished for what he has to say. He is only doing his duty."

"Very well. Say what you have been sent to say. I shall not harm you," the King of the elephants promised.

"Sir," said the little rabbit, "the Moon has this to say: 'You, the king of the elephants, have brought your herd to my holy lake and soiled its waters. You have killed thousands of rabbits on your way to the lake. You know that rabbits are under my special protection. I ask you not to kill any more rabbits. Otherwise something terrible will happen to you and your herd.'"

The king of the elephants was shocked. "You are right," he said. "We may have killed many rabbits on our way to the lake. I shall see that you do not suffer anymore. I shall request the Moon to forgive me for my sins. Please take me to the Moon."

The little rabbit took the huge elephant to the lake. There they saw the Moon reflected in the still waters. "There, your Majesty, meet the Moon," he said.

"Let me worship the divine Moon," said the elephant, and dipped his trunk into the water. At once the water was disturbed. The Moon seemed to move to and fro.

The rabbit said, "Now the Moon is angrier than ever."

The elephant bowed his head. "Please ask the Moon to forgive me. Never again will we touch the holy waters of this lake. Never again will we harm the rabbits that the Moon loves so much." And the king and his herd went back to their jungle.

Soon there was rain and the elephants lived happily. It did not ever occur to them that a little rabbit had fooled them.

Wisely said: Wit can win over might.

The Cat's Judgement

There, once, lived a bulbul in a deep forest who was very hard working. She had built a nest in a large peepal tree. She had been living there for many years. She was kind and all the little animals and birds were her friends.

One day, the bulbul left her cozy little nest and went in search of food. She travelled for many long hours. At last she reached a big field of jowar. It was harvest time and the jowar were fully grown. The bulbul was very fond of jowar. So, she ate as much jowar as she could. She made friends with the other birds who had also come there in search of food. She stayed in the field for many days.

While the bulbul was away, a rabbit who was in search of a home found her empty nest. The rabbit liked the bulbul's nest a lot. So he made it his home and started living there. He was very happy and all the birds and animals around became his friends.

When the bulbul came back, she got very angry to find the rabbit living in her nest. "Who are you? Why you are here? This house belongs to me," shouted the bulbul.

"Your house?" said the rabbit in surprise. "This house is mine now. I have been living here since many days."

"How can you live here?" asked the bulbul. "This house is built by me and I have been living here. If you wish, you can ask the neighbours."

The rabbit refused to ask the neighbours. He said, "I found this house empty, so I moved in. The house belongs to the one who lives in it and this house is mine now."

"No, this house belongs to me," cried the bulbul. "I had gone for a few days to find some food. Now that I have come back, will you please give me my house back?"

"No," answered the rabbit, "I shall not give you your house back at any cost. I shall stay here forever."

Both quarrelled for a long time. Many animals and birds gathered around. They listened to the bulbul and the rabbit. But none of them could decide whether the house belonged to the rabbit or to the bulbul. The animals decided that they must consult a judge to solve the dispute. But finding a good judge was not going to be easy.

The rabbit and the bulbul walked for hours to find a good judge. Finally, they reached the other side of the jungle.

There, seated on a big rock, was Manu the cat. He was very wicked and dangerous too.

When Manu the cat saw the rabbit and the bulbul coming, he pretended to be praying with his eyes closed, standing on his hind legs. In his hand he held a string of prayer beads, and he began to take God's name in a very loud voice so that the bulbul and the rabbit would hear him.

The bulbul and the rabbit were very much impressed on seeing Manu the cat. They found him humble and a

devotee of God. They decided to make him the judge for their dispute.

"But we must be very careful," said the bulbul. They waited till Manu the cat finished his prayers.

"O holy sir, a little quarrel has taken place between the bulbul and me. It is about an important matter of law. Please judge who is right and who is wrong and punish the guilty," said the rabbit.

"My friends, never say such a wicked thing. It hurts me when I see others in pain," said Manu the cat. "Those who harm others shall be punished by God. Now please tell me what your quarrel is about."

"This is what happened," said the bulbul. "I had gone in search of food for a few days. When I returned, I found that this rabbit had moved into my house."

"No, it is my house because I have been staying there since many days!" exclaimed the rabbit.

"Please keep calm, both of you. Let me hear the whole story," said Manu the cat.

The bulbul told him the story in detail and so did the rabbit. Manu the cat patiently heard their story and closed his eyes for a few minutes. Then he spoke, "Listen friends, I have become very old. I can neither hear you clearly nor see you well. So will both of you please come closer to me and narrate the story again?"

The rabbit and the bulbul, who were no longer afraid of Manu the cat, moved closer to him. Instantly, the cunning cat pounced and killed both of them. He then proceeded to eat them up and satisfied his hunger.

Wisely said: Solve your problems without getting into more problems.

A Wise Advice

Ramu and Shamu were good friends. Both of them were woodcutters who stayed near the woods. One day, they went to the woods to cut trees.

Shamu began to boast about his bravery and told Ramu, "I am not afraid of wild animals. I can kill them with one stroke of my sharp axe." Ramu heard this and said, "That's very brave! I am proud to have a friend like you."

Suddenly, they saw a black bear coming towards them. On seeing the bear Shamu got so scared that he ran and climbed the nearest tree, leaving Ramu alone.

Ramu did not know how to climb a tree. He thought, "Now what should I do? I have heard that bears never touch dead persons. I'll try and save my life."

The bear was approaching fast towards Ramu. He quickly lay down on the ground pretending to be dead. When the bear came near him, Ramu held his breath and kept as still as a dead person. The bear circled around him and smelt him. Thinking that Ramu was dead, the bear left and walked away into the woods.

After the bear went, Shamu came down from the tree. He went and asked Ramu, "Hey Ramu, I saw the bear whisper something in your ears. What did he say?" Ramu answered, "The bear indeed gave me very wise advice. He told me to never trust a friend who boasts about himself, for he shall leave you at the time of difficulty." Shamu was ashamed of himself as he realised his mistake.

Wisely said: A friend in need is a friend indeed.

The Poor Brahmin

Once, there was a poor Brahmin who was living in a small town. He was so poor that he never wore good clothes, or indulged in the luxury of eating. He had matted hair, an unshaven beard and uncut nails. He was extremely weak and emaciated because he had no cover from cold, sun or wind or rain. Taking pity on him, a rich man donated two calves to him.

With all care and love, the Brahmin fed the calves well with butter oil and grass. The calves grew into two fine and healthy animals.

One day, a thief saw the calves and thought to himself, "I must somehow steal and sell them. They will bring me good money." That night he set out for the Brahmin's house. On the way, he saw a lean but scary figure with dishevelled hair, loose teeth as long and sharp as fangs, an arched nose and blood-red eyes. Though he was frightened, the thief asked him, "Who are you, sir?"

"I am a monster. Who are you and where are you going at this late hour?"

"I am a thief. I am going to steal the calves of the Brahmin."

The monster trusted the words of the thief and said, "I take only one meal a day in the evening and I will kill the Brahmin for my dinner."

Both of them went to the Brahmin's house. When they were sure that the Brahmin had slept, the monster stepped in to kill the poor Brahmin. The thief held him back saying, "It is unjust to kill the Brahmin before I can take away the two calves."

The monster said, "If the sound of the resisting calves disturbs the sleep of the Brahmin, I will not be able to kill him."

The thief replied, "Suppose if you will face some problem in killing him, then I will not be able to take the claves. Therefore, wait till I finish my job first."

The thief and the monster began quarrelling about who should be the first to act. The Brahmin woke up due to the commotion they were making and asked them who they were and what was the matter.

The thief pointed at the monster and said, "O Brahmin, this monster wants to kill you and make you his meal."

The monster denied and said, "O Brahmin, this thief wants to steal your calves."

The Brahmin quickly invoked his deity through prayer and the power of the prayer forced the monster to flee. The Brahmin then took a stick and drove off the thief.

Wisely said: When your enemies quarrel, you are the winner.

The Sage and the Mouse

Once upon a time, a sage used to live in a temple. He would go into the city for alms and in this way, he supported himself.

When the sage had finished his meals, he would put what was left over in his begging bowl and hang it up on a tree. Then he would go to sleep. In the morning he gave this food to the workers, who in return cleaned and swept his living place.

One mouse found the hanging begging bowl. Unknown to the sage, he would jump high and reach it without any difficulty. He would take away some of the food to his house. In this way, he enjoyed the food night after night.

When the sage noticed that his food was being stolen, he hung his begging bowl still higher. However, the minute he went to sleep, somehow, the mouse managed to reach the begging bowl and did as usual.

Finally, the sage thought of a plan to put a stop to the mouse's mischief. When he was wide awake, he would beat the begging bowl with a split bamboo stick to frighten off the mouse.

When the mouse felt that the sage has gone off to sleep, he would try to reach the food as usual. But the sage would wake up and hit the begging bowl again.

The mouse would run away as fast as he could but come back again after some time. In this way, both would spend the entire night, fighting.

One day a mendicant, who was on a pilgrimage, came to the temple to visit the sage. The sage welcomed him with open arms and invited him to stay at the temple.

Before going to bed, the mendicant spoke about religion. But as the sage was thinking of the mouse, he kept hitting the begging bowl with the split bamboo stick. He was not attentive to the mendicant and so he gave only abstract and absent-minded replies. The mendicant became angry and asked the sage to explain such behaviour.

The sage replied, "You are my dearest friend. Please listen and I shall tell you the reason for my lack of attention." He continued, "Every day, whatever is left over from my food, I put in a begging bowl and hang it high on a peg. But there's a mouse that, somehow or other, manages to reach it. He takes away some of the food that I give to the workers. As a result, in the morning there is not enough food for the workers and they refuse to clean the place."

"Do you know where the mouse lives?" asked the mendicant calmly.

"No, I do not," said the sage.

'Well," went on the mendicant, "this mouse, wherever he may be living, must certainly have accumulated quite a lot of food, and this gives him a feeling of exaltation and consequently the energy to jump so high." He said further, "Do you have a pickaxe?"

"Yes," replied the sage.

"All right then," said the mendicant, "I have a plan for tomorrow. Go to sleep for now."

Early next morning, both the sage and the mendicant followed the mouse's tracks, found his hole, dug up his store of food and took everything away. The mouse was not in his hole at that time. When he came to his hole, he found that there was nothing left for him to eat."

That night, when the sage started hitting his bowl,

the mendicant smiled and said, "My friend, don't worry. After losing his hoard of food, this mouse will also have lost his energy to jump high. All creatures react in the same way."

After the two slept, the mouse did come again but as he had not eaten any food, he did not have the strength to jump high enough to reach the bowl. Though he tried hard, he missed it and fell to ground. He became so upset that he stopped coming to the sage's place and went off to some other place.

Wisely said: Strike at the source of the enemy's power to destroy him.